The
SCRIBE'S
Letters

BY: ALAN BRENTS

www.xulonpress.com

THE LETTERS

Introduction

" $\mathcal{W}$ hat is truth?" Long ago, a man of great power and influence asked that question while not being aware that he was speaking to the only person uniquely qualified to answer it. Most who voice that question are stating a position rather than truly seeking an answer. The avalanche of implications behind those three words, "What is truth?" reveals much about the questioner. Chief of which is usually a desire to muddy the waters of clear thought, thereby allowing one to stand at the buffet of so-called "truths" choosing whatever is appealing at the moment. It is not my aim here to engage in intellectual gymnastics concerning the existence of truth. We will leave that discussion for another time, and for the moment stand on the solid foundation that deep down in the place of bare honesty, every person knows Truth is. The question we are all born longing to answer is, "What is the truth?"

The search for "the truth" is the quest that has marked and dominated my entire life. Consciously admitted or not, life is a continual series of decisions predicated upon whatever one perceives as truth in the moment. Almost all of what we cling to as truth is given to us by others. Parents, teachers, mentors, books, videos, and pictures, these are the lawyers that present their evidence and attempt to convince us of the truth as they know it. The elephant in the room is that though all see in part, we do in fact look through a glass darkly.

Speaking for myself, I was blessed with a brilliant mother who, though she left this life when I was quite young, planted within me an insatiable desire to know real Truth and an assurance that those who seek eventually find. Being cut from such cloth, I set my feet on a path that could well be described as more than forty years of searching and testing the best ways to serve God and to live a life pleasing to Him. Just as shooting at the wrong goal does not help much, even if you make it, I finally realized my whole focus was wrong. I stopped trying to appease God and began getting to know God Himself.

This new direction brought me to an entirely different place in my relationship with the Truth. Many who read this may get spiritual hiccups or become uncomfortable when others talk of knowing God or of the fact that God speaks to them. Without going over a much be-labored point, let me remind us all that Jesus Himself said, "My sheep know My voice." Just as I recognize the voice of my lovely wife because I have spent time to know her, I can discern the voice of the Holy Spirit easily when I look to Him, expectantly listening with spiritual ears seasoned and trained by time in His presence.

Receiving answers to great questions is often a long and difficult process for me. I am not sure if that is just the way it is, or if I should carry a sign that says "slow man working." I take encouragement, however, in the words of George Washington Carver who said he asked God for the secret to the universe and God answered that knowing the secret of the peanut was enough for now.

What you are about to read is deeply personal. This small book has been an emotionally painful journey, begun after an extended period of praying, fasting, and continually asking God to reveal to me what He is like and some of how He sees things. The chapters that follow are written as though they are the diary of an angel in heaven. Now before I am placed in the stocks and branded a heretic, please understand that the manner in which this book is written, especially the point of view, is a literary device. I am not claiming to have been to heaven, or to have received an angel's private writings. I am simply attempting to shed some light on Truth by looking at it from the other side.

With that in mind, please read on after considering a thought that I am convinced God revealed to me—a thought which launched this entire process. Imagine, if you can, an evening of overwhelming grief in which you sit quietly weeping with the knowledge that tomorrow your children will die by their own hands and you cannot stop it.

Dedication

*T*his work is dedicated to my mother, Jo Ann Brents, who left this life at too young an age but before she left, she taught me how to ask questions.

Acknowledgements

*S*pecial thanks to our friends Rick and Cindy Mooney, two of the best examples of Christ on this earth.

Thanks to Rick Renner who mentored me in the early years.

My eternal gratitude to my three sources of never-ending inspiration: Valerie, Heather, and Austin.

And most of all, thanks to my precious wife, Sharon, my true north in this life.

Endorsements

"*A*lan Brents writes a delightful story from one of heaven's own perspectives. From the creation of man, to the dark hours on the cross, to the anticipation of His return, we are invited to see how heaven sees and observes Love Himself. You will smile and you will shed a couple of tears in this story of wonderment, as the author beautifully depicts the heart of the Father for His kids." Barbie Johnson, author of <u>Common Choices for Uncommon People</u>

"Alan is a story teller and doctrinal teacher rolled into one!" Melva Lea Beacham, minister of the gospel of Christ, psalmist, missionary, author, and conference speaker

"Wow! Alan's stories always come from a unique point of view, unlocking biblical truth in a way you would never expect. The results are an entertaining and engaging yet profound revelation of God's Word!" Chris Barnard, Business School and Third Year Intern Coordinator for Charis Bible College

Letter One

When God Wept

My name is not important. My position is. I stand in the court of Almighty God, in the very presence of the Eternal One. Since my day of dawn I have remained here. I worship—how could one not? I listen, I observe, and I engrave upon living stone the record of all that happens here. I am a scribe, but to be more precise, I am <u>the</u> scribe.

Every moment here is filled with almost unbearable glory. We call this place the throne room, but that is not an accurate label. The word "room" does not even come close to describing this vast expanse. There is no discernable ceiling or roof above us, and I have never spoken with anyone who has journeyed far enough to find any walls around us. I will do my best to relate a little of what we experience here, but true understanding does not even begin until one is here in person. Even then, eons will pass before it is possible to take in the beauty around us. The vast crystal sea reflects deep and intense colors that no artist has ever imagined. Music flows like massive, overwhelming rivers from the instruments and voices of the worshippers. What's more, and this will be difficult to understand, the sounds can be seen. Worship and praise flow all around us, in us, and even through us—and our eyes can actually see this. Here, dance and movement are breathtaking and constantly new. Creativity is everywhere like the atmosphere around us, the air we breathe. Worship here is not just performed; it is experienced. When dancers leap, every heart rises with them. Every note is heard and felt by all. As singers fill the air with loveliness that brings laughter and tears at the same time, the song seems to come from everyone and everywhere. Before I become completely lost in trying to describe what is considered normal where we dwell, let me return to the task at hand.

Worship here is not just done, it is experienced!

Recent events have taken turns both wonderful and terrifying. I struggle to relate our amazement as we watched the Creator of all design bring into reality a new universe. Where once there was nothing, there is now a mysterious place full of stars, and planets, and immeasurable possibilities. Granted, it is quite small and finite in size, but I find a kind of condensed beauty that mimics heaven itself, in a miniaturized way. My curiosity was piqued as He placed a beautiful blue sphere in one out of the way corner and took such great care forming and shaping it. We were all delighted as the Father lovingly covered it with life of every kind.

Then, to our utter astonishment, a new creature we had never seen before began to take shape. Til this moment, living things of all kinds continually appeared in a whirlwind of creation. We delighted as animals and insects of every color, shape, and size paraded before us. Then suddenly, the Master Craftsman slowed. All understood the importance of what was about to be done. We looked on as the Living Word began to sing and the ground where He stood began to stir. From that dust, a tall figure stood as God released life into it. I thought it quite amusing to notice as the Father of all Life breathed out, we all caught and held ours. Such simultaneous surprise was unavoidable when we all realized God had made this creature in His own image! Then sometime later, in answer to an unspoken question, He brought forth another one from the first, different and yet the same.

What happened next I still cannot fully comprehend and I can only relate to you what I saw and heard. The Great I Am, the personification of Love Himself, announced, "These are My beloved children and I grant them their own will. They will love Me only when, and if, they choose."

"These are My beloved children and I grant them their own will. They will love Me only when, and if, they choose."

We all responded with stunned silence.

Even though we had no understanding of any of these things, this concept stood out from the many other new concepts we had never experienced. For example, consider darkness. None of us had known this was possible. Somehow the Origin of all Light had divided the light from the dark and called the opposing forces day and night. Thus began my marking of entries into the record with this new creation called time.

The days that followed consisted of one adventure after another. We all remained quite busy watching and helping God's precious ones explore and learn as they walked and played with the seemingly endless variety of animals and plant life in this beautiful place. Each evening God Himself walked with them in the garden He made for them. Talking, laughing, teaching, and just being together—was truly wondrous to behold!

Yesterday, however, something changed. I had no idea what it was, but something was different. All appeared unchanged and familiar yet somehow slightly strange. What had been solidly balanced felt almost imperceptably tilted. Like a faint sound I could not quite hear, the perfect peace of this place now rippled.

As the dark began to reach out and push the day aside, the Everlasting Light slowly returned to His throne. Sitting in awesome splendor, the Author of Joy began to eminate what can only be called grief. Deep, immearsurable grief began to flood the far reaches of eternity. Wave after wave of stifling, horrible anguish swept over us all. We were drowning in a sea of unbearable pain that should have destroyed all there is, and would have, if not for the Father's ever present grace and mercy.

After what seemed an eon of time, I prepared to write for I knew the Living Word was about to speak. With a heavy heart and a trembling hand, I wrote the three words He spoke: "Tomorrow they choose."

While night passed on the earth, we held vigil in the heavens. We waited, we prayed, and we pondered in silence. God wept.

Daylight finally came to the garden, and we all rushed to the ballisters of heaven to see what would happen. Two things were immediately apparent. First, Adam and Eve were walking together toward the trees. When I say trees, I mean the two trees the Gardener planted in the midst of Eden: namely, the Tree of Life and the Tree of the Knowledge of Good and Evil. The Tree of Life held every promise and hope, while the Tree of the Knowledge of Good and Evil held the power to separate one from the spiritual realm. Many angels had heard God instructing man to never eat of the fruit of that tree because it would bring death.

The second observation we all made together brought a collective gasp. In the branches of the forbidden tree, perched the one we had all known as Lucifer. Once he was the beautiful musician who stood before the Throne and led the entire kingdom in worship. But Lucifer made himself the enemy of us all. Oh, he had taken the form of one of the creatures of the garden, but we all knew it was him. Our distaste at seeing this vile being was instantly forgotten as the forlorn cry of grief surrounding us increased and intensified. Everything in me wanted to scream "No!" as God's two precious children turned toward the tree where the Deceiver waited. Suddenly everything made sense, as I realized to my horror that man was choosing death instead of Life, darkness instead of Light, himself rather than everything.

The next few moments are indescribable, for the pain was too great. After it was over, man, the crown of God's creation, disappeared from view. As one, all of heaven turned to see the face of the Truth. We were once again taken aback to see not anger or grief, but rather, determined resolve and something I can only describe as a new dimension of love—if that is even possible.

The overwhelming silence was broken by Michael and Gabriel asking together, "What will now be done?"

The reply was immediate and strong, "I will crush my Son."

The archangel Michael replied, "This is as Justice requires. Man must be destroyed."

"You do not understand," spoke the voice of I Am "As Love and Justice both require, the Son I speak of is Myself."

Letter Two

When God Smiled

We wait, we look, and we listen. With emotions rising and falling like the tides of a celestial ocean, we anticipate the turning of the first page of the Great Redemption Story. All things large or small, great or insignificant start somewhere. Whether event or living being, everything outside of God Himself has an "in the beginning." In the vast universe of God's creation, life always begins with a tiny, almost imperceptable conception. Just as a great flood can be traced back to its first raindrop, so also an all consuming fire spreads from a single spark. The orchestra tunes up and prepares to play. I am eager to savor the first note of the concert.

The mysterious plan of man's salvation is, for the most part, still hidden in the mind of God. I, myself, have recorded the Words of the Almighty explaining His design for man to "seek Him and perhaps reach for Him." There is an unfathomable depth of sorrow betrayed by the word "perhaps" in that simple statement. As angels serving the throne, we carry out assignments and complete our tasks. From these, we piece together vague speculations of the Grand Design. From the brief glimpses our various activities provide, a shadowy and distant path emerges. The one thing we know for certain is that the Spirit of Love longs for the flicker of flame that will signal the start of it all.

From one man, He made all the nations that they should inhabit the whole earth; and He marked out their appointed times in history and the boundaries of their lands. God did this so that they would seek Him and perhaps reach out for Him and find Him.
Acts 17:26,27

So we wait, we look, we listen, and we patiently search for the one Son of Adam to place His foot upon the path and thus take the first step of the journey back to the Garden. We are not the only participants in the hunt. As we are all too aware of the hordes of hell straining to discover the instruments of their assured destruction. Though from on high the fallen ones appear to be little more than a nuisance, on earth they can be quite inconvenient and unpleasant for man and angel alike.

There have been occasions when we were convinced the first seed had appeared. From time to time the Lord of the harvest would speak to one person or another, but as they listened and even at times responded, disappointment always followed as we realized something was still missing. That a huge blank space continues to accompany all of man's attempts at obedience so far is obvious. What is not so clear is what exactly is lacking. There are as many guesses as there are minds in heaven; but of this I am certain none, save one, possesses the true knowledge we seek. Of this one more item I am also sure; in due season, all will be revealed.

The difficulty is that man has tumbled so far down the dark well of separation that recognition of anything beyond what they see, feel, or taste has become quite an infrequent occurence. I must admit there are moments when all seems hopeless, but when one stands in the Presence of Hope Himself, there rises up the unshakable assurance that the remnant will always surface. Just as with the man Noah, someone always answers the call. There is always one who, though he cannot see, chooses to believe. Again and again courageous individuals have risen to obey heaven's instructions. We have watched, cheered, and even assisted as some of Eve's children have chosen to turn away from their own desires to follow after the inner voice they right-fully recognize as Truth. All of these have believed and many have acted upon that belief. But all, so far, have turned toward the One we know to be Love Himself with downcast eyes and faces hidden in shame.

Once, not so long ago, the first two concealed themselves from us in terror, expecting judgement and death. All those born since struggle in the morass of self-loathing, attempting to escape the gaze of the righteous God they constantlly misjudge.

Most have lived in constant and quiet desperation. Some have converted their frustration into a pretense of anger, shaking a tiny fist at the heavens all the while trembling inside with the same fear of impending doom.

What began in the garden with Adam's thinly veiled attempt to dodge the blame for his failure has become man's self-created religion. If you will recall, Adam's words were, "it was the woman <u>You</u> gave me," thereby turning the accusation back toward his Creator and Father. Adam's descendents now continually perpetuate the deception of crediting God for everything that happens, good or bad. They blindly stumble through life as if they did not possess a will, free to make their own choices with consequences of their own making. How can children, whose not so distant father walked and spoke with God in the Garden, be so mistaken? How can they not know the Truth upon which all truths rest? One who claims to know God is deceived if he does not comprehend that no one—not man, nor even angel—is ever forced to love another. Especially if that other is Love Himself. Love by its very nature cannot be coerced. A gift is not a gift if it is expected or required. True love can only be received when it is given freely without restraint or obligation.

True Love can only be received when it is given freely without restraint or obligation."

My pen has waxed deeply thoughtful as I attempt to relate the story that marks a point of demarcation at which everything turns. Wisdom admonishes us to "despise not small beginnings." The great truth hidden within that phrase is that all beginnings are small. At times, they are almost imperceptable. The moment man's journey home began was so mundane we almost missed it. The fact that man would be provided a door, a path, and an opportunity to return has never been in doubt. First. we knew God's very character would somehow bring grace into the equation. And secondly, on the day Adam and Eve left the garden, the foundation for restoration was begun. Most missed the significance of the Father's promise to set the flame, His own Holy Spirit, and the sword, which we call the Living Word, to guard the path to the Tree of Life. Think of it: they do not guard the gate to keep others out, as many suppose; they guard and maintain the path to the Tree of Life. The path is clear. What we almost missed was the quiet creaking of the hinges and the thin shaft of light that pierced the darkness as one man finally found the door.

Our brave hero's name was Abram and the great chasm he crossed was not even noticed on earth. Abram began by listening for and obeying the Spirit's voice telling him to leave what he knew and search for the city whose founder was Truth. Abram's response to what he could not naturally ascertain was laudible but not unique. Others before him had followed the promptings of the spiritual kingdom and aligned themselves with the purposes of heaven. Man, in his present state, was not capable of communicating directly with Almighty God. It was believed that if humans were to come into the glorious light of His presence they would be instantly destroyed. Because of this, the Object of our worship created ways to speak to these wayward children He loves so dearly. The wall of separation is thick, but it is possible to pierce through to deliver what is needed and required.

The ongoing conversation that opened between Abram and his Creator must have been terrifying to one of such limited capacity. Regardless of how his flesh may have responded, Abram persisted in his pursuit of God. Through blood, and fire, and unimaginable light wrapped in thick darkness, the Giver of Life revealed promises so great that I am amazed Abram could grasp them, much less believe them.

I find great difficulty in attempting to describe the extent of the reaction in the heavenly realms to this interaction between God and man. Astonished is not a word that would do justice to relate what we felt as we watched God seal a covenant in blood and even mark Himself in everlasting remembrance to the agreement made with Abram. Spiritually speaking, everything that matters concerning Abram changed. Even his name was made new: he was now Abraham.

At this point, I did not yet understand what made this relationship unique, although we were all aware it was somehow different. What appeared to be occuring was some sort of negotiation between perfect God and fallen man. And somehow the Greater One was doing all the speaking for Himself—and for the lesser party as well. At the conclusion, God placed the guarantee of the convenant and the requirements to be fulfilled totally upon Himself. That one act placed the promises made into an unbreakable state, making them sure and as good as done!

Through the years that followed, the Giver of Gifts brought mankind along the path of return by working through the faith of just one man. Simply because Abraham believed Him, God was able to give Sarah a son and supercede the natural law with the laws of faith. Through that same conduit, many precedents were set in place which would permit later events to occur. I now understand the significance of the day on the mountain when the hand of an angel stopped Abraham from sacrificing his son, Isaac, and doing in the flesh what he had already completed in the Spirit.

I'm curious. Have you discerned it yet? Have you discovered that singular condition for which we had waited centuries? What made Abraham's faith different?

I recall the moment well. Some of us had gathered amidst those tasked with watching the path to the Tree of Life. The discussion was lively as we bantered back and forth, unpacking various theories concerning the illusive missing ingredient. All we knew for certain was that we had received the instruction "you will recognize it when you see it."

In the place where angels abide, there is a constant flow to the tangible Presence around us. The subtle changes within that flow alert one to coming events. I can still feel the sense of anticipation growing all around us as we observed Abraham listening to the still small voice of the Spirit.

Like parting clouds, the light suddenly broke through as we all realized the truth of what was taking place together. Abraham's face glowed with joy, not fear; with peace, not concern. How I didn't see this coming, I have no idea. I should have realized it would be love! Abraham was the first to see the goodness of God and to let his reckless desire for that love overcome his fear! I immediately recorded the words the Eternal One spoke as He said, "I could not give what they would not receive." As I glanced up from my writing, I sensed all of heaven brighten and begin to rejoice. My heart warmed within me and my face grew wet with tears of joy as the One on the Throne turned to us and smiled.

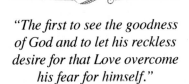

"The first to see the goodness of God and to let his reckless desire for that Love overcome his fear for himself."

Letter Three

When God Became Man

*R*eligions of men are like silly games being played by foolish knights while the castle walls are crumbling and enemies pound down the gates. Early on we were amused as men invented rituals and rules intended to grant them access to the reality they could no longer see. These poor deluded souls seem to think that if they afflict themselves with enough difficulty, the path of discipline will somehow help them reach the heavens. I ask you seriously, how can any intelligent being believe that such repetitive nonsense has any impact upon that which is eternal and immeasurable? I assure you such superstition is as effective as facing a hurricane and imagining one can turn around a few times, jump up and down, and by such actions change which way the wind blows. These worthless activities have taken root among men and grown past the point of disaster. No longer are they merely an attempt to touch the spiritual. Now man-made religion has become a great evil through which all of mankind is becoming enslaved.

During those first few intoxicating days of creation, man stepped forth in the newness of life. The first two of their kind, they represented a unique expression of the Father's infinite capacity to astound and amaze. The most intriguing aspect of it all was God's choice to create a three part being similar to Himself. Humans were crafted as spirits, real and everlasting, just like us, with minds to think and emotions to feel. Possessing a will that is all their own is what set them apart. To make the control of their destiny truly free, God kept Himself mostly hidden. Though He constantly speaks and interacts with them, a veil has been placed between the flesh and spirit. Without that separation, man would simply be overwhelmed by His presence and the choice our loving Father built into creation would disappear. To even exist without seeing the kingdom seems impossible to us, but every child is given the gift of the substance of faith. It is through that very faith that they are able to touch Reality.

The One who knows the beginning to the end placed all this wonder in a somewhat fragile shell fashioned from the soil of the place where they now dwell. One of the more frustrating consequences of Adam's choice at the trees was the realignment of his understanding of his own life. The spiritual blindness that accompanied leaving the garden caused man to now view himself primarily as the physical body in which he temporarily resides. From the vantage point of the Spirit, all things of substance are easily discerned. Existing outside time tends to make what truly matters stand out like bright planets against the inky blackness of space. But, apparently, to those trapped in physical flesh, these things are anything but obvious.

Therein lies the problem. The imperative challenge now is to somehow bridge the great gulf that separates Adam's blind children and the Divine. As I see things, it is impossible for anyone to cross from there to here. Consequently, a way must be found to connect here to there. The present consensus in my circle is based on the content of a number of messages about to be delivered to various souls on the planet. Everyone senses something great is about to happen and I believe God, the Son Himself, will descend to begin the process of repairing the breach. It

"It is no secret that every resident of heaven has been focused on restoring man to the garden from the day he left."

is no secret that every resident of heaven has been focused on restoring man to the Garden from the day he left it. What has not been known is how this will be accomplished.

Let us turn our attention to the events as they occur in the lives of the key players in this unfolding drama. To grasp the impact of what I am about to relate, one must understand the far reaching destructive effects of the self-righteous, ill-conceived religion previously mentioned. At this point in history, the revelatory voice of God had not been received by mankind for hundreds of years. Most people never even think of seeking truth or searching for any connection to spiritual reality. Instead they stumble along, entrusting the eternal welfare of themselves and their children to a few unworthy leaders. Rather than being servants, those pointing the way are blind leaders of the blind whose sole purpose seems to be establishing position and solidifying their own unquestioned authority. They are wicked shepherds who do not love the sheep; and because of that the flock is hopelessly lost.

There are exceptions however. A remnant always remains. Although sometimes buried beneath an avalanche of worthless dirt and rocks, flecks of gold can still be found. These are the souls who, despite the darkness surrounding them, still seek the source of Light. They may be unable to perceive even the slightest illumination, but they still cling tenaciously to the hope that somewhere a flame still burns. It is to these precious ones that so many of us are preparing to deliver the words of the Eternal. To some, the message will be instructional: do this or go there. Others will receive warnings of future events and some will be given life changing knowledge with which they will make far-reaching decisions. Many will simply share in the Great Good News.

We begin with one serving in a temple performing priestly rituals of worship. His name is Zacharias and though he is carrying out his ceremonial duties perfectly, his thoughts are far away. From his constant prayers, we know that he longs for two things: first that his beloved nation returns to the One True God; secondly, that his childless wife, Elizabeth, bears a son. Though he is quite persistant in his requests, I see little evidence of real hope in his heart. Concerning the first desire, Zacharias knows all too well that there must be a righteous voice raised up to speak forth the call. And he is just as convinced that there is none qualified to take up such a mantle. As to the deep longing to be a father, Zacharias is well aware from what his stiff bones tell him every morning: he and Elizabeth have grown old. Not ancient, mind you, but nonetheless past the childbearing years.

Suddenly, the old man's whispered prayers fall sharply silent. Every speck of darkness flees the room with furious urgency as Gabriel, the Archangel, appears standing beside the altar. When Zacharias leaves the Holy Place, he is unable to speak, but not for the reason you might suppose. To receive an angelic message from God Almighty answering one's deepest desires would indeed be enough to silence most. However, this diminutive priest could not restrain himself from blurting out his unbelief. If you understand the importance of words, even those spoken from ignorance, you will understand why Gabriel silenced the voice of doubt. The father of a child who would become the voice in the wilderness, preparing the way for God's promise, would not be heard again until after Elizabeth delivered their son, John.

Once again, excitement becomes a tangible atmosphere as Gabriel begins preparation to deliver another pronouncement. Being in the presence of an Archangel creates quite a stir of emotions. Those who dwell close to the throne walk in a level of humility that is impossible to explain. That very depth and peace of spirit makes others quite comfortable around them. I have observed many who are perfectly calm right up to the point at which they suddenly remember that they are standing near one of the most powerful beings ever created.

A rather large escort gathers to accompany this message. Apparently Gabriel is delivering something of great importance. When words of this kind are spoken to people on the earth, it is usually done alone and by a single visible angel. Just one heavenly messenger materializing from thin air is enough to shatter the resolve of most any normal person, let alone an entire cohort or in this case almost a legion. As always, Gabriel's escort will remain hidden from view to all but the enemy's foul servants who will no doubt flee the presence of so many shining ones.

We have learned Gabriel's destination is to a young girl named Mary in a tiny village called Nazareth. One would think that regular people leading quiet lives would not be noticed in view of the grand scheme of great events moving entire nations. However, the truth is quite the opposite. Consider the fact that the forces that move things spiritually are vastly different from those that impact events of note in the fleshly realm.

> *"Consider the fact that the forces that move things spiritually are vastly different from those that impact events of note in the fleshly realm."*

Accomplishing anything remembered and celebrated among men takes immense human effort,
ingenuity, and cooperation. While the crowds roar
and the victors congrat-
ulate one another, they
are hardly noticed here
in heaven. Here, what
matters is what matters.
True power is not con-
trol, manipulation, or
dominance over others.
How silly and small
those things appear

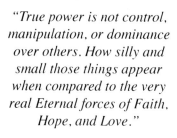

*"True power is not control,
manipulation, or dominance
over others. How silly and
small those things appear
when compared to the very
real Eternal forces of Faith,
Hope, and Love."*

when compared to the very real and eternal forces
of faith, hope, and love. Oh yes, my friend, when
some otherwise unknown child of God steps out in
faith, rest assured they have the attention of the
Eternal Realm. Much like a single voice singing in a
vast, silent room, we all know the names of those
who wield the awesome power of love.

No wonder we know Mary and how highly favored
she was with the Father. If you are ever present in
what we call holy moments, you will never forget it.
If the ground in heaven could quake, it surely would
have as Gabriel speaks with Mary. Even though we
well know all things are possible with God, I still am
often compelled to exclaim, "How is this possible?"
The questions pour forth in a torrent as, once again,
I am filled with awe and wonder as we worship the
One who knows beginning to end.

Soon after the knowledge of the coming child is
given to Mary, the message is carried to another. His

name is Joseph and he is to be the earthly father to the actual Son of God. Such a burden is without precedent, and Joseph's initial reluctance is understandable. Though the announcement brings great joy, I sense the underlying sorrow both in Gabriel and from the Father also. They alone know that this gift given to such tender ones as Mary and Joseph will bring much pain. Even while stepping out of Deity and taking on flesh, the heart of God is ever-turned toward these precious children He loves so much. No one could have foreseen God coming to man as a helpless baby: a conquering King or the Lord of Glory, of course, but a child born in the lowest of circumstances? Not in an eternity of lifetimes could one conceive it!

For those in attendance, the glory of that night is still fresh and will always be so. The picture of a soon-to-be father, fretting as he awaits the arrival of a new life does not fully express the intensity of that night in Bethlehem. Imagine, if you will, a tiny stable behind a small town inn. Though the inn is well lit and bustles with activity and raucous laughter, the animal pens are strangely quiet. In a corner of the stable yard stands a hastily erected shelter and within that tiny sukkah, a young mother struggles with the pains of childbirth while her husband prays in the flickering light of a small fire. Though Joseph and Mary may feel alone at the time, myself and quite literally millions of angels pace the skies and remind one another to breathe. Angels don't get nervous, or at least we tell ourselves we don't. But this night is as intense as it gets. We are not allowed to show ourselves except on specific assignments, but when the moment comes and the Christ Child draws His first breath on earth, nothing can contain the joy! The light of heaven bursts in the skies over Bethlehem. As far as the eye can see, the angelic host sings, dances, and worships the God of grace and mercy. Even the very stars and planets begin to sing! Unable to restrain themselves, some angels begin to shout the news to those awake in the fields around town. The Glory of God in the Highest is revealed, and His peace and good will toward man are released.

It is impossible to overstate the importance of this event. The Savior of the world is born. Men will call Him Emmanuel meaning God with us. And rightly so, for the Son is given, the Child is born. The Son could not be born, for the Son exists eternally. He has always been and He will always be. The Child, however, has not existed and therefore is born. God Himself, the Creator of the universe in all His glory, has become man.

> *"Emmanuel" "God with us"*
>
> *"God Himself, the Creator of the universe in all His glory, has become man."*

39

Letter Four

When God Wrote

*M*y heart is filled. Like an open sail straining at the ropes, stretching every seam to the limit, I try to catch and hold the infinite joy radiating from the Father. This is not one of the good days or even some special moment. This is normal here; it is like this all the time. How do I describe the indescribable? What words can I engrave that will somehow paint enough of the canvas to be recognizable to those who read this account? Once again, I must retreat from the attempt and trust that those who read this have also caught a glimpse of His glory and therefore understand. For truly, if one's eyes have not been opened by the Light, then the real world of the spirit is but dim shadows and hazy movement on the other side of the curtain. Here, where the paradox makes sense and immovable objects coexist with irresistable forces, the more one looks into what cannot be seen, the clearer everything appears.

Today is a day of days for us; especially for me. On this day, we are given another glimpse of a small part of The Plan. We are allowed to read another paragraph in what we have come to call the Great Redemption Story. It is always easiest for me as the scribe, to see our loving Father as the Author of all stories. I suppose if I was one of the players of musical instruments, I would be most keenly attuned to the music that sprays like the mist of a great waterfall around the throne.

On a side note, speaking of waterfalls, I was recently pondering how best to describe what it is like to look upon the face of God. I would be foolishly wasting my time and yours to try to relate the glorious mystery we experience when we look upon a countenance that is Father, Son, and Spirit separately and simultaneously together in one moment both loving and terrifying. The closest metaphor that I can give you is to consider a giant waterfall that is as tall as the sky and stretches from side to side as far as the eye can see. From a great distance, the scene appears tranquil and still, as in a painting. As one draws nearer, however, the movement becomes apparent and the closer you get, the wilder and more overwhelming it becomes. Magnify that experience many, many times and you will just begin to barely touch what it means to come into the Presence of the Almighty. I could camp here to talk about this for years, but with your permission, I will return to the discussion at hand which is the amazing events of today. As you have by now no doubt discerned, I find it difficult to stay on task to discuss anything without being drawn into attempting to describe some aspect of God Himself. All else pales when compared to the glorious rapture of His presence, and I'm sure you will forgive my wandering off into worship from time to time. Just as I was speaking of not being a musician, I suppose if my responsibilities were tending the gardens or leading the dancers or singers, my concerns and focus would reside in those subjects. I am, as previously stated, a scribe, a writer, a tradesman whose tools are words and sentences; paragraphs and tomes. Imagine my excitement when today, for only the third time, the actual hand of God wrote upon the stones of earth. First let us consider the import of the event itself. There have been many occasions when the Spirit of God has inspired men to write messages, instructions, and even whole books—thereby revealing His divine will to men. Only twice before has the actual hand of God appeared on earth and written a specific word. There are moments when the Eternal One does something so incredible that all of heaven holds our breath in rapt attention, and yet God's very sons and daughters walk by as if little has occurred. Just the rarity of the event makes this day especially important, but when we consider the actual message written, the significance becomes apparent and cannot be overstated. As I wrote earlier this was truly a "day of days."

We here in the heavenly realms have long understood that the story told about an event contains the same power as the event itself. In other words, whenever we describe or reiterate what God has done, we experience the same power He released when accomplishing the original occurrence. This is the key to a much discussed prophecy known here in the kingdom but not yet released in the world dominated by Satan. The first half we do not yet understand, but the second is clear "they will overcome the enemy by the Blood of the Lamb and the word of their testimony."

Words are powerful things. They can be used to instantly change the atmosphere in any situation. Spoken words can encourage the poor in spirit, heal the broken-hearted, bring freedom to those held captive or proclaim and release the Lord's favor in any situation. Faith-filled declarations can comfort those in mourning and even provide all that's needed for those who grieve, bringing beauty out of ashes and praise from the place of despair.

Words are like containers of energy and it is of the utmost importance when, how, and by whom they are used. This astounding and yet terrifying power can be transferred and even sometimes delegated

"Words are like containers of energy."

"The most powerful force available to man is the written Word."

by recording those words. In fact on earth, which is of course the focus of my records as of late, the most powerful force available to man is the written Word.

God Himself is infinite and eternal, and when looking forward from our perspective, He seems wholly unpredictable. Yet in hindsight, all that He does makes perfect sense—which places us in never ending cycle of "what?", "aha!", "of course." He does everything by divine law and eternal principle. Thus when all the pieces are in place, order reigns and every seemingly unconnected event is perfectly logical and right. In the end, everyone sighs with clear understanding and some even pretend they knew it all along.

Now I am sure if I were sitting beside you as you read this account, at this point the temptation to demand I tell you what has happened today would become unbearable. So I shall, but you must be patient, for the walls cannot be placed before the foundation is laid; and I have never been one to use ten words when a thousand would do just fine.

So as we continue our tale, let us examine the other two times God wrote upon the earth. The first was both predictable and understandable. Mankind had reached a point of wandering in a malaise of self-loathing wrapped up in conceit, barely even aware of his need for something greater outside himself. Into this darkness, the Eternal Light broke upon the man, Moses, and revealed to humanity their utter need for redemption when God's own finger engraved the Words of the Law upon the mountain of Sinai.

Although mankind was given the law and clearly told all that was expected, most of them continued in apparent blindness, seemingly incapable of understanding their unavoidable predicament. The inevitable warning that God does indeed know the hearts of men and weighs them on the perfect scale of righteousness came during a night of drunken revelry in a king's palace. The prophecy of doom was witnessed by those present as a disembodied hand wrote upon the wall, "you have been weighed in the balance and found wanting."

I trust that the implications of these events are not lost on you curious reader, for their meaning is both solemn and far reaching. The law is obviously perfect and perfection is the requirement for entering the Kingdom of our Lord. Man however is now absolutely incapable of keeping that Law and so we ask the question, "How is there any hope for him?"

This brings us to today. Mostly we here in heaven are only concerned with that which has eternal significance. Many times the small details of things that happen on earth escape notice. However, we here know that every thought, word, or action impacts whatever is around it, and that ripples on the surface eventually effect the whole body of water. With that in mind, let me set the scene for you.

Let us visit Jerusalem on a warm but pleasant day. Jesus, whom we know to be God's own Son, is quietly teaching in the temple. Those who have gathered to hear Him come from all walks of life and have but one thing in common. Though their outward appearance is as different and varied as can be, each and every one is driven by the same emptiness inside that cries out to be filled. Soon they are loudly disrupted by a group of men who do not wish to learn truth, but rather want to push away and even destroy anything that threatens their pitiful but comfortable self-righteousness. As these loud and boisterous men crudely push through the quiet crowd like bulls stomping through a small herd of scattering sheep, they shove before them a barely clothed and terrified woman who falls at Jesus' feet clutching a scrap of old blanket attempting to cover herself in shame. The obnoxious bulls begin to shout and challenge the quiet Teacher as He simply kneels. At this point, I jump up and focus all my attention on Jesus as He begins to write in the dust at His feet. According to these red-faced, self-appointed judges, this woman was the worst kind of evildoer. She has been caught in the very acts of her wickedness and the Law demands death for such as her! "What shall we do with her, Rabbi?", they loudly demand. Still, Jesus simply continues to write upon the ground. The impatience of this riotous crowd is quickly growing to an explosive situation, but all become suddenly quiet as the Son of Righteousness rises to speak. "Let he who is without sin cast the first stone," He simply says. It is then we notice what is in the hands of those cruel would-be executioners as the weapons of judgement are dropped to the ground with the sound of real, tangible shame. One by one every stone falls rattling on the floor of the temple courtyard. Slowly each accuser quietly makes his way out of the temple away from the pure gaze of Love Himself.

Now there has been considerable speculation about what is written upon the ground this day. Some say it is the law and others guess it is a warning and that is why the accusers left. But, we know that God had written these things in stone before and He does not needlessly repeat Himself. No, today was too important and heaven is celebrating as I can hear the sound of it all around me. All one has to do is listen to what the Son of Man, as He likes to call Himself, has

MERCY

been teaching for these last three years and combine that with the look of gratitude on the face of this poor woman to know that what God wrote on the temple stones today: was "mercy."

Letter Five

When God Danced

*T*hese earthly skies are filled. If the eyes of the people below us were opened to see into the real world, their hearts would fail them from fear. In my memory, we have never all gathered in one place and especially not for such an unthinkable reason. To merely consider the number of us is staggering. Words like massive, innumerable, or incomparible don't even come close. The very real weight of angelic presence is overwhelming.

I am amused to note the demon hordes normally flocking to places such as this are nowhere to be seen. For once, they have wisely removed themselves. Possibly they sense the coming destruction and fear being caught as collateral damage.

None of us have ever experienced or even imagined a day such as this. Is it any wonder that none could ever even consider the possibility that the Son of God would submit to being tortured beyond recognition? Who could foresee the Bright and Morning Star, the very source of joy, being horribly nailed to a cruel cross? The very people He came to save from death now demand that all of their wickedness be hurled at the One who is their only hope. The why in all of this completely escapes me, but of one thing I am certain: this tragedy must soon end.

We have watched men live and die for centuries. I have always been astounded at how tenaciously their physical bodies cling to life. Humans can endure incredible pain and suffering but no one has ever walked the dark path to this extent. I have seen the valley of the shadow; but this is no shadow. This is the real thing. We are watching death, darkness, hell, and every evil thing being poured out all at once on Love, Himself. Every fiber of all that I am is screaming, "This must stop now!"

All of the Angelic host, and I do mean all of us, await the command that will release us to end this horror. As much as we love these rebellious children and as fond of them as we have become, the full weight of heaven's armies is prepared to destroy them all.

> *"As much as we love these rebellious children, the full weight of heaven's armies is prepared to destroy them all."*

Warrior angels are a fearful sight even for us. I see them all together in full battle array standing rank upon rank thousands of legions deep. Their terrible swords are drawn as tears stream down determined stone-jawed faces. I tremble at the thought of what is about to come. We wait for but one word from the One who hangs before us suspended between the blood-soaked ground below and the dark, angry, weeping skies above.

All of these events are happening rather slowly. Yeshua actually hangs between heaven and hell for over three hours of time on earth. In the moment, everything seems to overlap in a jumbled up haze of frustration, anger, and bewilderment. In the immediate area around me on this small hill, seemingly insignificant events continue to transpire. We were so focused on Jesus that the laughter of the soldiers, the jeering of the crowd, and the weeping of Mary seem far away. I can see and hear them all, but it is like they are at the other end of a long tunnel. Yet as difficult as it is to believe, just a short distance away, men, women, and children continue on with daily life as if nothing out of the ordinary is occuring. Although all the spiritual kingdom has focused its attention on this moment, and even the earth itself is groaning with rumblings from the deep, most of mankind is totally unaware. As I have often observed, great events are usually accompanied by ignorance and apathy.

Once again my heart cries in anguish. Release us—let us stop this injustice! What purpose can this possibly serve? How can He let this continue? My questions fall unanswered on the stones of the Via Del a Rosa as the sky begins to weep with rain. My heart is breaking as the most precious blood of all runs down the rough timber to seep into the cursed ground below.

At some point in this hazy turmoil, I notice the heavens growing increasingly quiet. Visible light is fading as the sun itself hides its face from the little blue planet. Rivers of silent tears continue to flow from millions of angelic eyes as we strain to listen to what is spoken by the very Word Himself.

I stand close by the cross and am able to discern most of what transpires. I am astonished to hear God's only Son speaking with the two wretched things hanging on either side of Him. I'm sure few of us are even aware of these two men dying beside Jesus. Just as I begin to listen more intently to the labored conversation, our Lord turned His attention to one of them. I gather he is being executed for his crimes, and I think to myself how all of them deserve such a death.

Suddenly this barely alive thief gathers his remaining strength and pushes against the nail pinning his feet to the wood. With excruciating effort, he draws in what breath he can and gasps out, "Remember me when You come into Your kingdom." I must admit my heart breaks for this poor soul even as guilty as he surely is. Then I am once again taken aback as Jesus' reply is not what I expected. Although I instantly recognize the great love in His eyes, it is His words that change everything. Quietly, softly, and with no great fanfare, Jesus simply says, "This day you will be with Me in paradise."

Immediately three things happen. The overwhelming, thick silence that I had unknowingly been drowning in evaporates, as somewhere above me, the vast heavenly orchestra plays the first notes of the great song of rejoicing. Every part of my being shakes as does all the kingdom and even the earth below as Gabriel shouts, "THE FIRST HAS COME HOME!" While the quakes and tremors from that momentous announcement have not even begun to sub-

"The first has come home!"

side, the overwhelming sound of millions of voices raised in joy and laughter erupts near the throne as God the Father begins to dance!

Letter Six

When God Poured Out

*T*he almond blossoms have fallen. The rich green smell of spring is a faint, distant memory. I hear no laughter, once bright skies are moody and grey, and I sense no hope. In every place where men breathe, winter has come.

While earth weeps for what she has lost, heaven hums with overflowing joy. How could it not? The Bright and Morning Star, the one true King of Kings has returned home! Oh the glory of the day when the celestial gates swung wide and the Son once again sat at the Father's right hand.

I'm sure it is quite impossible to imagine the volume of worship in a place where the stones actually do cry out in praise. Since the moment He stepped out

> *"It is quite impossible to imagine the volume of worship in a place where the stones actually do cry out in praise."*

of the temporary and back into eternity, we have been lost in the beauty of His Holiness; whether mere seconds have passed or a millinium, I have no idea. All I know is He has returned to us and all is well.

In the midst of a celebration beyond imagination, I sense a tiny nagging thought that will not let me be. I attempt to ignore it, but fail miserably. The more I look away, the more it comes into focus. As I delve deeply into this heart of mine, I see a dimly lit corner and the faint pulsing of an unanswered question. I have no wish to acknowledge its presence, much less to voice my concern out loud. Anything based in truth or love, when suppressed, responds by growing stronger. And so while the Kingdom celebrates the homecoming of the King, unbidden tears silently slip from my confused eyes. One would think that when living endlessly in the presence of the Infinite Mystery, one would learn to expect the unexpected. One would indeed think that very thing—and one would be incorrect. I am still regularly amazed and surprised by the intricate twists and turns in the beautiful lace of eternity.

"Don't be distracted," I tell myself, "Just gaze upon the Source of Everything and your wandering thoughts will return to center." This doesn't work at all, for I find that the more intently I look to Him, the more concerned I become. Eventually I throw all caution and reason to the wind and look into the eyes of Love and I silently mouth the words, "How will they live without You?" My poorly timed, inappropriate question betrays how much I have come to love these lost children for whom the Son endured so much. I must admit, I am more than a little startled when I suddenly become aware that the One who knows the hearts of all is looking directly at me. I am both intrigued and elated when He says to me, "Remember and rejoice…remember what you have seen and rejoice for what you are about to see.

As it often occurs in heaven, I am neither isolated nor unique in the question asked and the answer I received. One of the wonderful things God often does is to speak specifically to one individual and yet to many in the same instant. Worthy is He who is both Three and One! Oh let us praise the glorious name of our infinitely mysterious God! Before I become totally lost in worship, I know I have not been the only one to hear His words. That fact becomes obvious as thousands of angels turn as one to watch what transpires among men.

To the uninitiated, observing earth from the vantage point of heaven would appear to be a daunting task. Consider the millions of souls with all of the tangled up web of emotions, thoughts, and activities that make up each life. If one tried to take all of that in at once, I cannot imagine the resulting confusion. We know that God Himself never misses even the tiniest detail. But I am thankful that He, never being the author of confusion, has designed the world in such a way that we may see and understand what is needed. Though the Creator sees all, the created do not. Unless on specific assignment, most of what happens among men passes unnoticed by the worshipping angels. Let a man, woman, or child step out of the ordinary and do something of faith however, and instantly all eyes are on that believing one.

It is that filter of faith, if you will, that draws all our attention to a large room where a number of those who follow Jesus have gathered. As we listen in, I conclude that just over nine days have passed since they watched the One who conquered death ascend beyond sight into the heavens. I remember that day well, for I was present on the mountain as the Risen One spoke to a large crowd. Curiously, most of those there then are not here now. In fact I would say only about half of half still remains. "Why?", you ask. I can only speculate based on the observation that man will sometimes choose to pursue a course that he knows full well will lead to ruin. Apparently the unfettered ability to choose life or death through faith in the unseen also allows one to believe or not believe even in the face of irrefutable evidence. If that sounds hard to swallow, let me assure you I have seen even the most knowledgable mired in self-deception. The Son of Man Himself once said, "If they will not believe My words, they will not believe one who returns from the dead."

"Remember"…this is our assignment and that is exactly what these weary ones still waiting here are doing. I gather from what I've heard so far, the last nine days have been one continuous struggle to get God's attention. After getting past the initial shock of losing Jesus for the second time, they set about attempting to receive what the Savior promised them. They beg and plead, shout and bargain—a long, loud yelling match that has finally run its course.

They sit quietly now, as one after another shares his or her story. The laughter brightens the room and the tears flow freely as they talk of the words Jesus spoke and the things He did. In the long moments of holy silence, they remember and peace comes. They remember and resolve is strengthened. While others just grieve, these remember. We watch thin hope

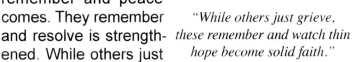

"While others just grieve, these remember and watch thin hope become solid faith."

become solid faith. I sense those around me leaning forward in anticipation for nothing captivates an angel's attention like hearing the stories of Jesus.

Everyone in this room has been touched by the hand of the Lord and changed in some way. That is the reason they are here and why they stay. Every tale is different and every soul is unique. But somehow they are all still the same. Remember what you have seen and rejoice for what you are about to see. I ponder these instructions as everyone begins to giggle and clap with glee when one man gets up and dances around the room. No explanation is needed, for by now all know he was once bound firmly to a mat on the ground begging for his very survival. Whether dry and dusty, or muddy and miserable, the lameness of his shriveled legs gave no hope of ever rising to breathe the clean air of freedom. But in a moment now celebrated with every leap and twirl, everything changed. Each step he takes is remembrance filled with uncontainable rejoicing.

Another man present always brings a knowing smile to the face of anyone he looks upon. For those shining eyes were once dark with blindness. I notice the slight conspiratorial wink and the grin that says, "I can see you."

Some of the women move among the group giving food with a word of encouragement and a tender touch. To the unaware, their small acts of kind contact might seem unimportant; but most in this place remember that the soft, smooth hands serving them were once twisted and horribly ravaged by leprosy. The unclean and ugly are now the pristine and beautiful. The blind now possess the keenest sight. And the lame and broken now leap and run ahead like children racing for a pool of cool water on a hot day. I remember and rejoice for the many lives that were changed in the last three years, but I can't help thinking of those who never knew Him.

Upon close inspection several oddities become apparent to anyone who has observed mankind for any length of time. Most obvious is the chaotic diversity of this group. Young and old, rich and poor, people from every walk of life are present. What's more, they don't seem to care at all about one another's status. The smallest child is afforded the same rapt attention and respect as the eldest statesman. All that seems to matter at this moment is, "What do you know of the Master?" The hunger to know more of Jesus is real and tangible in this room. I sense that yearning growing with every morsel shared. This gathering of followers is experiencing one of those mind-numbing mysteries that swirl around the Everlasting Presence like hungry children in the kitchen when bread is baking. Only in the Spirit can one be fully content, and yet still thirst—or be completely without need, but never lose desire. Not unlike the wisp of a vague dream that hangs just out of reach, true reality is sometimes quite unreal.

The conversation takes on a soft reverence when one called James begins to relate an account no one has heard before. With great care he shares what he and two others experienced recently on a mountain top with the Lord. Appearing with Jesus that day were two figures they knew to be Moses and Elijah. He said it wasn't till much later they realized the significance of the Law and the Prophets. But most amazing was when Peter suggested building three tabernacles to honor Jesus, Moses, and Elijah. A booming voice from heaven spoke saying, "This is My Son, listen to <u>Him</u>." With this revelation all understand why the story is difficult to tell. Few have been publicly and audibly rebuked by God Himself. A rather young lad speaks up and suggests that it seems as though Moses and Elijah are stepping off the stage and the audience is realizing the story was really all about grace the whole time.

A soft-spoken woman with beautiful, long silver hair talks of the Lord as a babe. She tells of Simeon, an old man who prayed and blessed the child; and how he prophesied his own welcome passing now that his own eyes had seen Salvation. She also remembers Anna who also blessed Jesus and His parents. At the time, Anna's strange prophesy about dwelling forever in the temple from that point on seemed odd to say the least. Eyes grew wide with wonder as many recognized Simeon symbolizing the law being fulfilled and Anna, whose name means grace, remaining forever. How intricately woven together is the fabric of this great tapestry.

The sayings and teachings of the Rabbi are repeated and savored like long overdue rain on a dry and thirsty land. Some of the more cryptic phrases He spoke are considered and pondered. For example, Jesus once told His disciples after performing an amazing miracle, "Greater works than these you will also do." And who could forget, "I go to prepare a place for you"? But the most incomprehensible was when just a few days ago Jesus said, "It is better for you if I go away." Even Peter, who always has something to say, was speechless at that. There is possibly no better example of the truth that His thoughts are not our thoughts.

That very statement, "It is better for you," stabs at the heart of what is bothering me and a few million of my closest friends. Man's only hope of salvation has defeated death and the grave, and yet for the last several days, He seems to have left them on their own. Yet these few hold on to the one simple instruction He gave them. Wait. I am sure we are missing something here, but what is it?

Though my heart thrills at the re-telling of every story, it also aches within me. Behind every precious face, these little ones are hurting. They have tasted Heavenly glory and now are ruined for the mundane. I can feel the keen sharpness of their longing for

Him. From the depths of desperation, they cry out for His presence. With reckless abandon they reach for Him.

Suddenly I'm startled with the realization that something is stirring around me. Yes, stirring is exactly the right word. A wind that is barely percept-able, yet huge and powerful, is slowly swirling around us. I am caught up in the moment as every faculty I possess trembles with ever-increasing intensity. What was moments ago a quiet breeze is now a full force gale. The depth and volume of what seems to be some kind of great storm is beyond description. I have not felt this much power since Jesus rose from death. Now much larger than even the created uni-verse itself, the wind roars like no sound ever heard before. Angelic beings all around me are awestruck as I feel myself vibrating like the strings of an instru-ment plucked almost to breaking. Above the over-powering, cascading sound the only voice capable of being heard thunders, "NOW!" To the utter shock and amazement of all of heaven, God Himself is standing over the room of one hundred and twenty open, yet empty vessels. Wave after wave of the Father's joy crashes over us as He pours out of His very heart, His own Holy Spirit.

Below us the former sons and daughters of Adam, stand with hands and faces upraised as fire descends upon each one. "Surely they will be con-sumed," I exclaim. But somehow they are able to receive it. As one, they all begin to give voice to the worship that overflows from their newly filled spirits.

The sound is easily recognizable, we hear it always around the throne, but never before on the earth.

Wonder of wonders—I thought that I had been amazed before this! So this is how they will accomplish all that has been foretold? He will dwell in them! As long as the Son was with them in the flesh, they were limited to His immediate physical presence. Now He is in them! No wonder He spoke of greater works. Nothing will be impossible for them. What are the schemes of the enemy compared to one filled with the very Spirit of Almighty God? No task will be too difficult, no mountain of evil large enough to resist. The very halls of hell itself will tremble in fear as these called out ones go forth. What a day! What a glorious day! Ring the bells of freedom for the chains that bind the captives are breaking! Let the poor hear the good news! The broken-hearted will be healed and those who are bound will be loosed! Proclaim it from every mountainside for the day of vengeance has passed and has now become the year of the Lord's favor! Let all who grieve be comforted! Give them beauty for ashes and the oil of gladness instead of mourning. Let all the world rejoice and cast off the spirit of heaviness and put on the garment of praise! What was once man's deepest desire—"God with us"—has been surpassed and become "God in us." Remember what you have seen and rejoice for what you now see. The Holy Spirit of God has been poured out!

"What was once man's deepest desire, "God with us," has been surpassed and become "God in us."

Letter Seven

When God Answered

There is a great difference between heaven and earth. In some ways, they are the same, but in most, they are vastly different. The Spirit of God Himself has told man on several occasions, "My ways are not your ways." All beings, man or angel, have the tendency to see things through the lens of their own point of view. Events, all observations, and the memories they engrave upon us are unavoidably colored by the sum total of who and what we are. In no small part, due to this fact, I'm sure you have noticed my tendency to remember from the point of view of who I am. I'm also just as certain, you, the reader, interpret these musings from the vantage point of your gifts, abilities, and experiences. These facts don't change Truth; they merely affect the way we understand and apply it.

One of the most difficult areas for those of us here in the real and eternally-present kingdom is our inability to comprehend mankind's apparent blindness to reality. Over and over again, we watch humans struggle with the most obvious and simple precepts. I have concluded that Adam's decision to connect himself to death lowered some sort of veil or curtain between him and the spiritual world. All of Adam's children for thousands of years seem affected by this limited sight. Even in their own writings, they describe it as looking through a transparent but darkly-tinted gemstone.

To make this even more frustrating, I have observed that certain truths cannot be passed on. What I mean is, one would assume that once a fact or observation about reality is understood, all people thereafter would receive and walk in its light. This is unexplainably not the way of things on earth. Some principles and even the very essence of man's relationship to his Creator and to us must be discovered individually by a seeking pilgrim. Day after day, we watch some precious one struggle up the mountainside of revelation, eventually finding that which he seeks only to watch others repeat the entire journey step by step to gain the same morsel of knowledge. The pattern is always the same and the result is usually very similar. Once the light of Truth shines, such a one immediately attempts to share it with everyone he or she knows. In most instances, this is met with disastrous results. Relationships are often broken and intentions are misunderstood. Although sometimes, very rarely, the seed of Truth falls on good, well-prepared ground and takes root.

These children our Father created are truly a curious and demanding lot. They are never satisfied to just sit quietly where they are with what knowledge they have. This is a good thing, for otherwise, they would remain in darkness forever, never knowing reality. Over the centuries, I have noted certain questions that must be common and basic to all mankind for they are repeated over and over again. We have come to call them the "universal longing." At some point in the journey, every human being must confront the question, "Why is there evil in the world?" Even more importantly all will wonder, "Why does an all-powerful God not stop it?" Most of the human struggle is predicated on the need to know the answers to these deep longings of the heart.

The truth is both simple and complex. All things are simple to the one standing on this side of the puzzle, looking back through the already solved riddle. The difficulty comes when one covers the eyes and attempts to hide from the Light yet still wants

"The difficulty comes when one covers the eyes and attempts to hide from the Light yet still longs to see."

to see. The solutions to these problems and the conundrums they seem to spin off such as, "How can a loving God allow a child to suffer from no apparent fault of his or her own?" can and will be explained. One of the most basic principles in play is "Those who seek, shall find." If you are already on the well worn trail of the great search, let me assure you there is an end to the journey and there is peace after the battle.

Now, as always is the case for those who search, curiosity and impatience are starting to barge in on your otherwise complacent demeanor. Nevertheless, let me remind you there are steps you must take and prerequisites you must complete before the room of understanding is well lit.

First, before I attempt to put flint to steel and flame to wick, I must qualify my tale with what I cannot say. Specifically, it is far beyond impossibility for me to explain how our loving Father restrains Himself from intervening directly in events so obviously contrary to His will and desire. Let it suffice to be said He does it somehow and that particular piece of knowledge is not pertinent, nor even relevant to the fate of mankind. The why of it all, however, is of paramount importance. Understanding why He relates to His children this way is everything.

After much thought and reflection, I have concluded that to set about imparting information to you, the reader, in the way of a professor in a classroom would produce the same result as the aforementioned analogy. Sleepiness and boredom would invade our conversation and understanding would only follow the sincere, self-motivated search embarked upon by yourself. Thus I have decided to borrow and relate the writings of another. It is my hope that as you travel with him along his painful journey to illumination, some of that beautiful glow will spill over onto your own path.

Most of what I've shared so far in this series of letters has been somewhat chronological from an earth-bound point of view. Although I've tried to hold your present limitations in mind as I've written, we will now skip a couple of thousand years forward as I share with you some pages from the journal of the man I mentioned earlier. Our time frame here is the late 20th and early 21st century with our youthful pilgrim being at about sixteen years of age. Keep in mind, I'm sharing only the highlights of what was a thirty-six year journey for him. Let the eavesdropping begin.

Journal Entries:

January 1973

> *Why, why, WHY!! The more I ask, the less I know. At church they all say what they always say, "God is teaching you something. His purposes are beyond understanding." And of course they always quote, "All things work together for good." Bull! Sorry, but I'm not stupid enough to just blindly follow all the catch-phrases that religious people say. It doesn't make it true just because it's on a poster or bumper sticker. I may be young, but I've been around long enough to know that saying it from a pulpit doesn't guarantee truth either.*

April 1974

> *Mom is worse today, much worse. I can't tell if my sisters know and I don't think my little brother has a clue. Who knows what Dad thinks; he lives in his own world of pain and doesn't let anyone in there. Never has.*

July 1974

> *I always thought that good things happen to good people and bad things to bad people. If things went wrong, then somehow you deserved it. This makes no sense. Mom is the strongest, most loving, and giving Christian I know. I've always thought if God would heal anyone, it would be her. But we've been losing this war with cancer for years. She's been through so many procedures, I can't even remember them all.*

September 1974

> *Once again, Mom asked us kids to come and stand beside the rented hospital bed we set up in the living room for her. I griped about it the whole time, but I really know what she is doing. She is trying to memorize our faces so she can remember them. She's going blind.*

February 1975

> *God is in control." If I hear that one more time, I'll scream! Sometimes they say, "God loves you," or "Remember Jesus loves you" in the same sentence. Morons! All of them!*

April 1975

> *Another late night sitting up talking with mom. How can such calm words come from someone in such pain? Her mind is still as brilliant as ever, which is surprising since her very brain is being destroyed by cancer.*

July 1975

> *She's blind, can't see a thing. Last Saturday, I put on a blind fold for a couple hours to see what it's like. As bad as it was, I always knew I could take it off and see. Can't imagine the horror of never ending darkness.*

May 1977

> *Had a long talk with mom tonight. Wasn't sure if I should go to Colorado this summer or not. I feel like I'm supposed to go and work at a Young Life camp, but I know she doesn't have much time. Mom thinks I should go anyway so I'll hope for the best.*

June 8, 1977

> *Funeral today. Don't remember much; just that the whole world's gone quiet and dark.*

July 1977

> *Why? The question still remains. Why did this happen and where was God?*
> *Everyone seems to be so sure of their answers, but the more I hear the more I'm convinced that they are all wrong.*

August 1978

> *Dear God,*
> *I've walked this path seeking you for more than 10 years now and there are some things I know for sure, but they don't seem to fit together.*
> 1) *I know that You loved us so much You were willing to die for us.*
> 2) *I know that You are interested in me personally not just the whole world.*
> 3) *I know that what You did was not just to get us in heaven. I'm not sure how but somehow there is a way to interact with You, right now, here, today.*
> 4) *Somehow, I will discover the truth. If I do nothing else in this life, I will leave it knowing why the heavenly Father I love and serve would sit by and let such evil win.*

The death of this young man's mother was a long, drawn out process of endless prayers and tears. The very real miracle in all this, so far, is that he did not walk away bitter and angry which is usually the case. As we skip forward several years, we find him as determined as ever to find the truth that seems just out of reach.

Journal Entries:

January 1984

> *He allows everything! It's not the whole truth, but it's a major part of it. We always pictured God as sitting up on the throne protecting us from most stuff, but then letting other stuff through from time to time just to teach us something. How blind could I be? To let us have free will, He has to allow it all. He accomplished all that was needed on the cross. We've been thinking the key was in getting God to feel sorry for us and get up off the throne and do something. He already did!*

February 1984

> *The new is worn off. The excitement I felt at realizing God allows everything is gone and now I must climb the next ridge and find out how to get God's very real power involved in my life right now. Is it possible, as some say,*

to walk so close to God that nothing bad ever touches you?

August 1986

Right now it's a little like writing a song. Small pieces of lyrics float around just out of reach as melodies come and go at the oddest times. All these snippets of revelations whispering in quiet voices are slowly coming into focus. "It is better for you if I go away." "Say to this mountain…only believe and do not doubt "Call things that be not as though they exist." "You shall know the truth." Patience tells me that the mist is clearing and soon I will know.

March 3, 2013

Yesterday, I sat in a deserted emergency surgery waiting room while people I do not know cut open my beautiful wife of 28 years. Tears of hopelessness and fear wrenched my soul without mercy. I was advised to prepare myself as her condition did not give much hope. Statistically, she faced overwhelming odds toward death and little chance at life. I must admit, I was not the great, strong man of faith that I've always thought I was. Wilted, broken, and weak was rather how I would draw the self-portrait. Then late last night in ICU through the darkness, the light of God's Word began to speak. The first loving admonition was soft *but firm, "sorrow endures for the night, but joy comes in the morning." Instantly, I knew that my Father had allowed my one day of panic, but now it was time to go to work. Tentatively I quietly asked the question, "Are you going to do something now?" So many scriptures and truth went off all at once as Love Himself cried out in my spirit, "I gave My Son, My Word, and My Spirit; how long will you allow evil to triumph? It is time for <u>you</u> to stand up and fight the enemy!"*

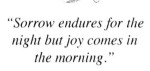

"Sorrow endures for the night but joy comes in the morning."

Since I don't want to leave you hanging, I will say that our stubborn seeker and his precious wife did fight and win that battle and many others. They also learned another great truth along the way. Walking in the light of the Word does not mean that bad things don't happen; on the contrary, one becomes a bigger target for the enemy. Soaring to such heights however, does mean a life of moving from one victory to another in the ever increasing knowledge of faith. What should you take from this true tale?

If you seek, you will find.

If you knock, He will answer.

Letter Eight

When The Lion Roars

I am not a warrior, or rather I should say I'm not classified as a warrior angel since war and battle are not my primary purpose. Be that as it may, we are all warriors from a certain point of view. As you know, I am the scribe who stands in the Chamber of Origins where all things begin and end. My reason to be is to record all that our Father says and does here. The ever-expanding hall of remembrance is filled with countless living stones upon which I have inscribed the events of the ages.

There are few things as glorious as watching the plans of our Eternal Commander unfold before us. Although we rarely know the entire plan or even the purpose of what we're doing, there is usually a moment when understanding dawns, the seemingly unconnected pieces fit, and suddenly everything makes sense. Recently we experienced one of those moments of enlightenment in an area that has puzzled us all for a long time.

I will attempt to convey this newly discovered truth. However, in order to do so I must first shed some light on the war for men's souls in which we are currently engaged. Yes, there is war in the heavenlies and it is constant. This conflict is quite different from the banishment wars when Satan fell like lightening from his place of honor to the very depths of despair. There are certain similarities, however; the most obvious being we are battling the same enemy. It is interesting to note that although this struggle is fought with different weapons and for different reasons, the opposition is just as desperate.

As I have said, I stand in the very Presence and I record all that is spoken. It is impossible to describe the voice of God and there is nothing more wonderful and thrilling than the sound of it. The very essence of life is in the words our loving Father speaks. He uses words to create, to love, to instruct, and to share some of Himself with us and man.

At times the Almighty One speaks directly to man and at other times He sends a messenger to convey His thoughts. It is this communication with man that brought about this mystery of which I now speak. Obviously it is an immeasurable honor to be given the task of carrying a message from God to someone on earth. There is always much excitement accompanying the preparation for such an event. An angel speaking directly to a human is not a simple affair. You see, the bearer of the treasure of God's very words and the warriors assigned to go with him must enter the arena of our enemy. Oh yes, perhaps you've forgotten that the earth is temporarily dominated by Apollyon and his minions. This means a visit to the blue planet will most likely involve a battle against a desperate and wicked foe where, for us, failure is not an option. Do not misunderstand. The enemy does not war against Almighty God; they learned the utter futility of that long ago. Satan has, however, turned all of his insatiable desire to kill, steal, and destroy towards God's children and His angels.

We have learned from our encounters with humans that apparently we appear quite fierce to them and we are always required to reassure them we have not come to destroy, but rather to assist and serve. It is a great tragedy that Adam's sons and daughters have drifted so far from reality that they are shocked and afraid upon encountering the all-encompassing spiritual kingdom built upon the very foundation of Love itself.

It is the process of delivering these messages that has all of us here so perplexed. While we see the necessity of unveiling pieces of the plan to certain of God's children, we are understandably reluctant to reveal any information to the demons who are always listening. However, our all-knowing God has made a way as He always does.

What now seems so simple was once so confusing, especially at first. To grasp the significance of what I'm about to tell, you must understand that for thousands of years, since man was removed from Eden, all of the resources in the vile kingdom of darkness have been aggressively applied toward discovering the identity and location of the promised Savior of mankind.

Some twenty centuries ago the voice of God had not been heard by man in over four hundred years. Gabriel was sent to tell a priest named Zacharias that his wife would bear a son who would be the forerunner to the prophesied Messiah. All went as planned, but we were amazed when the demon hordes who surely heard the announcement reacted with confusion and chaos. We observed this same strange response when Mary was told she would bear the Christ Child and when the truth was revealed to Joseph. Most incredible was the obvious lack of understanding among the principalities and powers of evil at the great and unmistakable pronouncement to the shepherds in the fields when all the heavenly hosts could not contain themselves and spontaneously broke into songs of praise. Consider our astonishment when time after time God Himself or one of His angels would speak clearly upon the earth and yet all of hell would react with nonsensical foolishness.

It was some thirty years later that understanding began to peek through. Jesus, whom we all knew to be God's own Son, was being baptized by John in the Jordan River. As Jesus came up from the water, the Father's unmistakable voice clearly spoke the words, "This is my beloved Son in whom I am well pleased." Some of the people there at the time understood every word, but others were confused and thought it was thunder. This same thing happened again and again with the same mixed reaction from those present. God's words would be delivered, and some would hear clearly and others would hear thunder or the wind or a kind of great rumbling noise.

It all made sense on a day some years later right after Jesus had returned to us here and we all stood by as God poured out His Holy Spirit on a group of one hundred twenty precious ones who had gathered and waited. As God began to fill and speak to each one all at the same time, an amazing thing happened. All those in the city outside began to hear a sound like the roar of a great rushing wind. This was so unusual thousands gathered in the street to discover the source.

"The roar of a great rushing wind," I thought to myself. of course! He is the Lion of Judah; it must be the roar they hear. The source of all Truth looked back at us and smiled for He knew we had discovered another secret and He was pleased. That explained the mystery. While those intended to receive a message from heaven understood it, even though they did not always believe it, those to whom the words were not directed heard the roar of the Great Lion! It also explained why Satan seemed to continually be strutting around pretending to be some great roaring beast who can devour anything in his path. How small and foolish he looks compared to the real thing.

With all that in mind, let's jump ahead to the present where all of heaven is abuzz with anticipation. Two thousand more years have passed and the still small voice and the sound of the wind have been heard time and again in the lives of those who are listening. We are all aware that these are the last of the last days before the Great Homecoming and God is about to release something new and powerful in the earth.

Today we have gathered at the rails of heaven in barely contained anticipation. We are waiting for the One who spoke all into existence to speak once again. All heaven cannot contain the glory as the Holy One rises from the throne. I think of the places on earth where the faithful have gathered seeking grace and longing to hear His voice. All eyes turn and focus on those precious believing, trusting, seeking children. I feel the rumbling begin deep and incomprehensible as my heart stirs within. Once again I see the Father smile and I feel His joy. Every part of my being trembles as He says to us "Prepare yourself...THIS WILL BE LOUD!"

About The Author

*A*lan Brents and Sharon, his wife of thirty years have two daughters and a son, a son-in-law, and three grandsons. Alan and Sharon love to minister the Truth of the gospel of Christ to people and help them see who their identities in Christ really are. They take each opportunity to go and minister to those who need to know that they are truly loved by God Himself. It is Alan's heart to see many come to know Jesus as they receive Love Himself and walk in the power of God's Word.

Alan and Sharon have served in many ministries in the local church, which include pastor, worship leader, youth minister, children's minister and any other roles in which a need existed. To know the truth is to be set free.

Alan can be contacted at eabrents@yahoo.com or at sharonbrents@yahoo.com

CPSIA information can be obtained
at www.ICGtesting.com
Printed in the USA
FFOW02n0120060416
23007FF

9 781498 447775